The Secret of the Leaves

by Esther van Handel
illustrated by Chagit Migron

 o one paid much attention to what Beryl had to say. Not that he didn't speak loud enough. Beryl spoke very loud. In fact, he yelled a lot.

One day in school, the teacher wrote questions on the chalkboard. The boy in front of Beryl stood up. Beryl couldn't see the board.

"SIT DOWN!" hollered Beryl.

But the boy didn't sit down. To make matters worse, instead of punishing the boy who was standing up, the teacher punished Beryl.

He had to write a hundred times:

We don't scream in class.

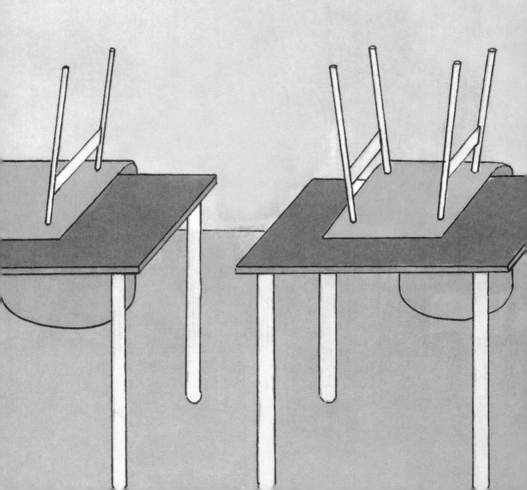

During recess, Beryl was playing ball with his friends Dovi and Shlomo. The ball flew high up into the sky, then dropped back down – right on Beryl's nose.

"WHY DID YOU THROW THE BALL AT MY NOSE?" screamed Beryl. "DON'T YOU KNOW HOW TO PLAY?!"

"Oh, stop hollering," said Dovi, as he threw the ball to Shlomo.

When Beryl came home, he growled, "I'M HUNGRY! I WANT SUPPER — NOW!"

Beryl's mother was so tired of hearing him yell all the time that she ignored him.

"Why doesn't anyone ever listen to what I say?" wondered Beryl.

The next afternoon, little Avi fell asleep. This was the opportunity Beryl had been waiting for. At last, he could build a big city without his baby brother destroying it. He took out blocks, people, farm animals, cars, and trains, and went to work. He built houses, playgrounds, stores, and a school. He built a farm to provide food for all the people and a road for the cars.

Then his big sister Sara came home from school. She walked into the room to put away her coat. All of a sudden, CRUNCH! Sara accidentally stepped on a house.

"GO AWAY!" shrieked Beryl. "YOU RUINED MY CITY!"

"I'm sorry," said Sara. "It was an accident."

This time Beryl yelled even louder. "IT WAS NO ACCIDENT! STOP MAKING UP EXCUSES!"

Beryl's shouts woke up little Avi. Avi climbed out of his crib and headed straight for Beryl's city.

"OH, NO!" hollered Beryl. "THE MONSTER IS COMING. HE'LL BREAK MY WHOLE CITY!"

"Me look," said Avi. "Cow say moo."

Avi reached for the cow, and the barn came crashing down.

Now Beryl yelled even louder. "MY CITY! YOU BROKE MY CITY!"

Avi began to wail.

Beryl's mother came running in from the kitchen. "Why is there so much noise here? Look, Beryl, you woke up the baby! Now you'll have to watch Avi for an hour so I can get supper made."

Beryl felt very sorry for himself. How could he keep a world champion trouble-maker out of trouble for a whole hour?

Beryl thought and thought. Then he had an idea.

"Mommy," he said, " May I take Avi for a walk in the park? He will like the trees and the grass and the flowers and the birds."

"Certainly, Beryl. That's a wonderful idea."

Beryl put Avi in his stroller. Mother gave them apples and crackers with peanut butter to take along, and off they went.

Soon they came to the park.

The park was big, shady, and quiet. Overhead, puffy white clouds drifted across a bright blue sky. Beryl and Avi smelled the flowers, turned somersaults in the grass, chased butterflies, and listened to birds sing.

Suddenly, a breeze whipped by. It sailed through the trees and gently shook the branches. The leaves rustled. Beryl and Avi stopped to listen to the delightful, soothing sound.

"Whoosh-sh-sh," went the leaves. It seemed to Beryl that the leaves were whispering a special message to him. "Do you want to learn our secret?" they asked him.

"YES!" shouted Beryl eagerly.

"Whooosh-sh-sh, speak softly. Then everyone will listen to you, just like you stopped to listen to us. Sh-sh."

"But I get angry," said Beryl. "How can I help yelling when I'm angry?"

"Whooosh-sh-sh, speaking softly will calm you and everyone else down," said the leaves. "Then you won't be angry anymore. Sh-sh."

Beryl thanked the leaves for telling him their secret.

"Whooosh-sh-sh, don't thank us, said the leaves. "Shlomo Hamelech — King Solomon — was the wisest of all men. He said:

דִּבְרֵי חֲכָמִים בְּנַחַת נִשְׁמָעִים

Wise people speak softly.

We learned this secret from him."

Beryl put Avi in the stroller and headed for home.

When they were right in front of the house, Avi climbed out of the stroller and sat down on the pavement. "No go home!" said Avi, stamping his feet. "Me stay outside!"

Beryl was about to yell at him. But he remembered the leaves' secret. "Avi," said Beryl tenderly, taking his hand, "we had a nice time in the park, and now it's time to go home. Please come with me."

Lo and behold! Avi came.

"*It works!*" thought Beryl.

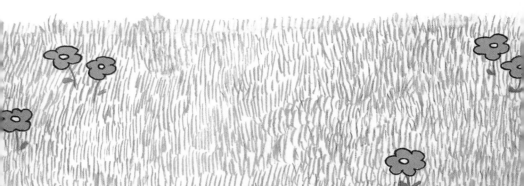

Beryl was very, very hungry after his long walk in the park. He dashed toward the kitchen. Suddenly he caught a whiff of kasha — the food he liked the least in the whole world. He wanted to scream.

But he remembered the leaves' secret.

"Mommy," he said softly. "Could I please have something else instead?"

Beryl's mother spun around in surprise. She could hardly believe her ears. "Yes, Beryl, since you asked so nicely."

Beryl smiled as he happily twirled spaghetti around his fork.

The next day, ten minutes before school ended, the teacher announced, "Boys, you've been learning so well that we finished the *Chumash* a whole week early. As a reward I'd like to take you on a trip. Is there somewhere you'd like to go?"

Dovi's hand shot up. "To the park. We can row boats and play baseball."

Shlomo objected. "To the zoo. We can see elephants and lions and monkeys and hippos and …"

Thirty boys began to talk at once. In the middle of the tumult, Beryl said quietly, almost in a whisper, "I think …"

Suddenly, the other children stopped talking. They all waited to hear what Beryl would say.

"I think we should go to the safari," said Beryl. "It has a park and a zoo."

"Great!" everyone said. "We like Beryl's idea."

Beryl beamed. "How lucky I am," he said to himself, "to have learned the leaves' secret."

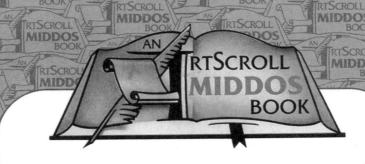

Good Middos are the good traits the Torah tells us about — traits which help make us better Jews and better people. If we have good *middos,* we will always act, and say, and do things in the proper way.

But where can we find good *middos?* No one sells them or gives them away. We can only acquire them by looking and learning, by watching and listening. And by practicing.

In the **ArtScroll Middos Books,** you will find lots of interesting, exciting, fun-to-read stories with beautiful pictures. Each story will help you learn something new and important about **good middos.**

Enjoy!